Churchill's
TALE of TAILS

Anca Sandu

JONATHAN CAPE | LONDON

To Joe, Sue and Abi for believing in me.

To my Mom and Loïc for their support,
love and an endless supply
of macaroons.

CHURCHILL'S TALE OF TAILS
A JONATHAN CAPE BOOK 978 1 780 08009 3
Published in Great Britain by Jonathan Cape,
an imprint of Random House Children's Publishers UK
A Random House Group Company
This edition published 2012
1 3 5 7 9 10 8 6 4 2
Copyright © Anca Sandu, 2012
The right of Anca Sandu to be identified as the author and illustrator of this
work has been asserted in accordance with the Copyright, Designs
and Patents Act 1988. All rights reserved.
RANDOM HOUSE CHILDREN'S PUBLISHERS UK
61–63 Uxbridge Road, London, W5 5SA
www.randomhouse.co.uk
www.randomhousechildrens.co.uk
Addresses for companies within The Random House Group Limited
can be found at: www.randomhouse.co.uk/offices.htm
THE RANDOM HOUSE GROUP Limited Reg. No. 954009
A CIP catalogue record for this book is available
from the British Library
Printed in China

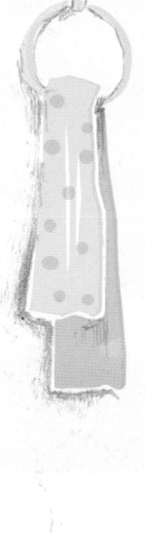

Churchill was a very proud pig,
just like any other pig. This is his

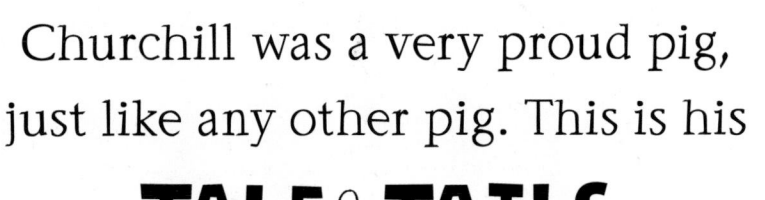

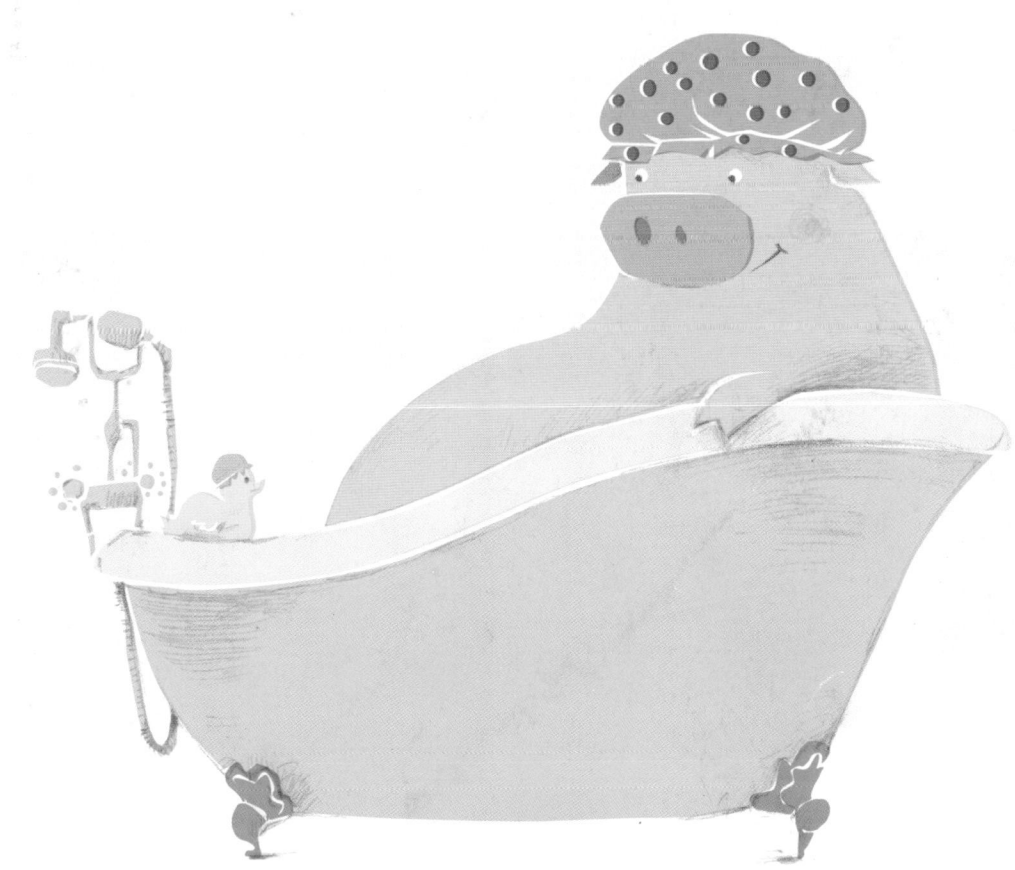

Churchill valued many things in life:

smelling beautiful flowers,

painting self-portraits,

playing classical music,

or reading a good book.

And he loved to have a cup of tea
with his friends, Billy and Gruff.

But Churchill had one
thing that he prized above
everything else ...

his tail.

It wasn't a big tail.

It wasn't a fancy tail.

It wasn't even a very practical tail.
But it was his tail ...

and it made
him feel great.

But one morning ...

his tail was nowhere to be found.

Churchill searched here,

there

and everywhere.

Finally, he gave up searching.
He was **miserable**.

"I just don't feel myself
without my tail," he said.

But Billy and Gruff
came up with
a good idea.

They gave Zebra a call.

Hello, Zebra, We have a tail emergency. Can you help?

Come over — I think we have just the thing.

The zebras were happy to help.
They had a spare tail
for Churchill to try.

But the zebra tail didn't feel quite right.
"Perhaps I should try some other tails," Churchill thought.

So he went to see Peacock.

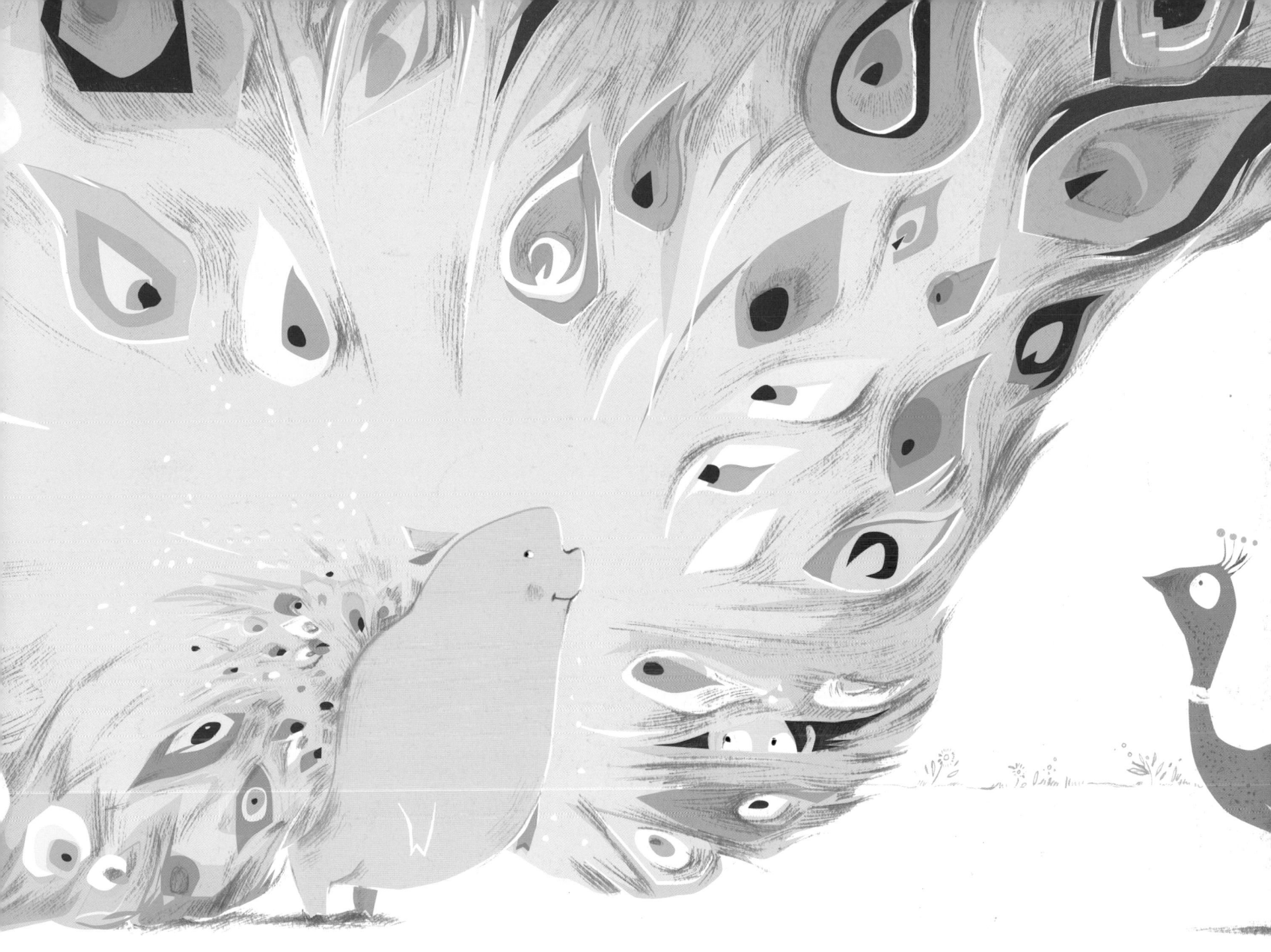

Peacock gave Churchill a tail that made him feel beautiful.
"Ooh," said Churchill to himself. "I wonder what other tails I could try."

A tail from the fish made Churchill feel **fantastic!**
He could do things he'd never done before.

Churchill never talks to us any more. It's all these fancy tails.

He tried little tails,

spotty tails,

snappy tails,

and tails that
made him feel
big.

Trying different tails made Churchill feel so good
that he didn't have time for anything else ...

Come and play,
Churchill.

not even his
old friends.

"NOW," thought Churchill, "it's time for something **VERY** special."

So he went to Tiger's house.

Tiger's tails were really super.
"I feel fierce!" said Churchill.

"I am the world's strongest, bravest pig," he said.
"I'm not scared of anything! I'm totally fearless!" But then …

Churchill felt terrified
and very alone.

What could it be?

A giant, mean lizard?

An unfriendly blue alien?

Or a huge,
hungry robot
with a twisted fork on its head?

But it wasn't any of those things.
It was just a little bird.

"What's that on your head?"
asked Churchill. "Is it my tail?"

"Well, I don't know," the bird replied. "I found it in a bush ...

I thought it
was a worm.

But I couldn't eat it.

It didn't look like a flower.

It was **useless.**
So I put it
on my head.
I've grown
rather fond
of it ..."

"Oh, but it is my very
own perfect tail,"
said Churchill.
"Please may I
have it back?"

"Well," said Bird, "if it's yours then you should have it!"
"Thank you," said Churchill.

Finding his old tail made Churchill
feel like his old self again.
He was so grateful that he
helped Bird find the perfect
thing for her head.

And making a kind new friend
helped Churchill remember his old ones ...

So he organised a tea party
to bring all his friends together.
"My dear friends," said Churchill,
"I have been a very silly pig, and a very
bad friend. Can you ever forgive me?"